The Basket Maker and the Spinner

Other Walker Books by Beatrice Siegel

Indians of the Woodland
A New Look at the Pilgrims
Fur Trappers and Traders
The Steam Engine
The Sewing Machine

Beatrice Siegel

The Basket Maker and the Spinner

Illustrated by William Sauts Bock

Walker and Company
New York

First published in the United States of America in 1987 by the Walker Publishing Company, Inc.

Published simultaneously in Canada by John Wiley & Sons Canada, Limited, Rexdale, Ontario

Library of Congress Cataloging-in-Publication Data

Siegel, Beatrice.
   The basket maker and the spinner.

   Summary: Tells the stories of the Indian basket weavers and colonial spinners of early America and discusses the preservation of their craft in a time of advanced technology.
   Bibliography: p.
   1. Indians—Basket making—Juvenile literature.
2. Basket makers—Juvenile literature. 3. Spinning—Juvenile literature. [1. Indians of North America—Basket making. 2. Basket making. 3. Spinning.
4. United States—Social life and customs—Colonial period, ca. 1600–1775. 5. Handicraft] I. Bock, William Sauts, 1939–   ill. II. Title.
E59.B3S56   1987   746.41′2′08997   86-32617
ISBN 0-8027-6694-3
        0-8027-6695-1 (Reinforced)

Printed in the United States of America

10 9 8 7 6 5 4 3 2 1

To my daughter Andra
and my granddaughter Julia
carrying on
the artists' gifts today.

Contents

Introduction

"Atisket atasket,
A green and yellow basket:
I wrote a letter to my love
And on the way I lost it.
I lost it, I lost it,
And on the way I lost it."

In the headlong rush to the modern world, we lost more than the letter. We also lost the basket, for modern technology has all but swallowed up the great art of basketry of our Indian ancestors.

If you can work a computer, do you care about baskets? If you can land on the moon, or if you can retrieve treasure buried in deep seas over hundreds of years, where does the basket fit in?

Still, like old memories, baskets linger on, and we like to look back to an earlier time, to the way the first people in this country lived.

Thinking of baskets for even a few minutes makes us pause in the heady race of today's world. We escape from the world's problems: problems of crime, drugs, pollution, and nuclear missiles. Baskets speak of a quieter, softer time, of communal caring, of patience and perseverance. Baskets bring back to us the inner solitude and artistry of Indian women whose role in thousands of years of the continent's history we have yet to appreciate.

The spinner also talks of an earlier time but in a different voice. Spinners were not native to this soil. They were the colonists who introduced European ideas and technology to the eastern seaboard.

Though the basket maker and the spinner had much in common, they told different stories.

The Leaves
Are Falling

The sunflowers stood tall and stately. They lingered in the garden like the last rays of summer sun. Yawata, looking over the land in the early fall, knew that the sunflower heads would soon tilt downward, drooping like a sleepy child. The nights were cooler, the days shorter, and the russet autumn leaves were falling. Sometimes the world stood still, but now all around her was movement. Flocks of ducks and geese, in flight to warm climates, filled the marshes. Often the sun itself was blocked out by thousands of birds migrating south.

Yawata also moved to the beat and rhythm of the world around her. She was a woman of one of the largest New England tribes, called the Wampanoag, and had been born and reared in the New England woodlands where native people had lived for ten thousand years. She was brought up from infancy to feel at one with her surroundings, to listen to the murmuring winds in the woods. Her strong straight body moved easily in soft leather clothes. A headband held

13

back her long straight hair. Under her feet, shod in soft deer skin *mocussinass* (moccasins), she felt the contour of every stone and the shape of the earth. Overhead the color of the morning sky announced the weather. Trees and plants gave her messages of the changing seasons.

Yawata's religion strengthened her ties to nature. She and her people had deep faith in supernatural forces and in the belief that spirits resided everywhere in nature: in animals, in plants, and in people. Spirits could be reached through an intermediary known as a *shaman,* or medicine man, a person of strong supernatural powers. Through special rituals and ceremonies, the shaman could call on the rain spirit to end a drought, or on the spirit that protected hunters; he took care of the sick, or kept a watchful eye on children, or guarded warriors during a war. Over these many individual spirits reigned the Great Spirit, known to the Wampanoag as *Manitou.* The whole living world was thus linked together, and every aspect of nature had deep religious significance.

Now that the leaves were falling, Yawata knew that she would have to dismantle her summer home. Her wigwam, like the others in the village, stood on cleared ground around the communal center. In back of the homes stretched acres of farm land.

In all the years of their long history, Yawata's people had moved from season to season to be near food. For the winter she would seek the safety of a warm, sheltered valley where men would hunt deer and other animals. They would also help build strong winter homes to withstand snow and sleet. Summer or winter, wigwams looked as if they grew out of the earth. They were made of saplings dug into the ground, arched over, and lashed together. Over the frame, women placed tree bark or tightly woven cattail mats that repelled rain. Indoors, mats were used for flooring, wall covering, beds, and seats. Loosely woven summer mats were often left behind with other household items too heavy to carry.

Though Yawata worked from morning to night she did not complain but accepted her role in the village and tribe. Her three children were now learning traditional patterns of work in which each one contributed to the welfare of the whole community.

This life style also made it easier for Yawata to get through the endless round of chores. She never worked alone, but in a group of women. Together they built homes and cared for them, raised the children, gathered and prepared the food, tanned skins, and cut and sewed them into clothing. They carried water and wood. They worked on clay for pottery and spent every available moment weaving baskets and mats for their practical needs. Perhaps more important than most of their chores was their work as farmers. Yawata's children, as well as other village children, helped their mothers in the planting, weeding, and harvesting of crops. Yawata's youngest daughter, six-year-old Quenimiquet, had a special task. She and other youngsters sat among the crops many hours each day to shoo away the birds.

Yawata's husband, a warrior and hunter, worked alongside other village men building canoes and making tools. They spent long hours shaping bone and stone into chisels, hoes, and knives.

The village center was the meeting place for women, men, and children. Here they relaxed and enjoyed themselves in athletic games and, sometimes, at gam-

bling. The center was also the gathering place for religious ceremonies and dances.

Over the years village women grew more kinds of vegetables and harvested bigger crops. Sometimes they produced more food than the men did in winter hunting. Maybe someday women would grow enough farm produce so that they could, if they wished, live in one place. Then Yawata would be able to live year-round in her village, near her vegetable farm and the sunflowers.

Though it was now fall, Yawata paused in her round of work to think back for a few minutes to early spring, to the month of March, when the sap flowed in trees and spawning fish filled the rivers. That was when her whole village camped in the woods near the maple trees to tap them and make sweet syrup.

Then came *Sequanankeeswush* (late April and early May), the month "when they set Indian corn." The land had long ago been cleared for farming. Into small mounds of earth women placed both corn and bean seeds. Between the mounds, they planted squash, pumpkin, and peas. This year Yawata planted sunflowers, while others planted Jerusalem artichokes. By harvest time, the garden plots were a tangle of greenery. Bean vines were curled around corn stalks for support while pumpkin vines crept along the ground. But the women and children who cared for the crops every single day knew exactly what was going on. They carefully weeded, removed harmful insects, and shooed away animals and birds.

Maize, or corn, the staple crop, had multicolored kernels of white, red, blue, and yellow. Starting in August, the first ears of corn were picked and placed on mats to dry in the sun. At night, women covered

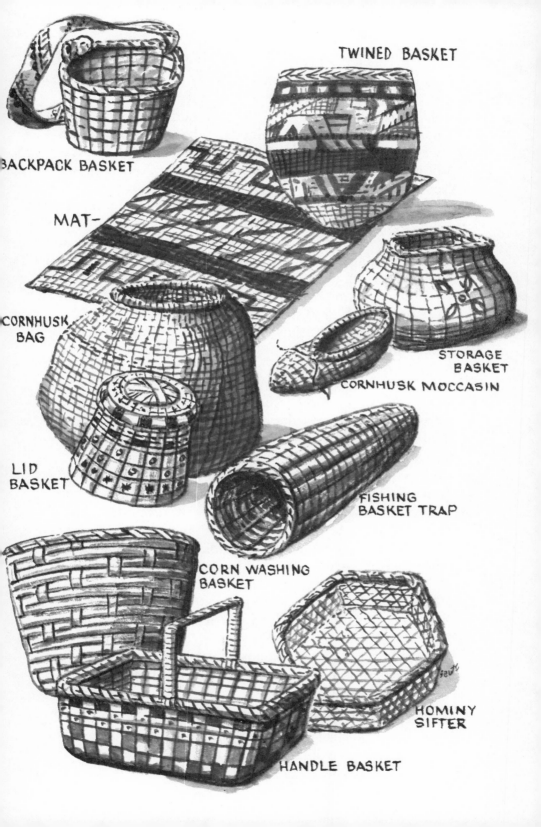

TWINED BASKET

BACKPACK BASKET

MAT-

CORNHUSK
BAG

STORAGE
BASKET

CORNHUSK MOCCASIN

LID
BASKET

FISHING
BASKET TRAP

CORN WASHING
BASKET

HOMINY
SIFTER

HANDLE BASKET

the corn with more mats for protection against both dampness and hungry animals. When dried, the corn was placed in large baskets and hung on walls of the home to be eaten whole or beaten into flour for pancakes and bread.

Hanging on the wall in other baskets were dried nuts and berries picked during the summer.

Yawata and other village women were in charge of the home and the food supply. They regulated how much corn could be eaten and how much had to be stored over the winter until the next spring. When families returned to summer lodgings, and until the first harvest in August, they lived on fish, wild berries and nuts, and the food carefully stored in deep baskets in underground pits. These deep holes in the earth were padded with mats to keep the damp earth away from the baskets of food. Additional mats were wrapped around the baskets themselves to protect them from rain and foraging animals.

Mats and baskets! They were used for everything. For storage; for pots, pans, and dishes; for bags and boxes. There were baskets for trapping, fishing, and hunting; for cradles; for carrying water; and for cooking. They came in all sizes and shapes: giant sized or tiny, round or square, with handles or not, covered or not, flat or deep, soft in texture or stiff and firm.

Stored in Yawata's home were wild grasses, cattails, twigs, and strips of bark ready to be woven into baskets. But Yawata was not unique. The world of basketry belonged to women along with all their other work. Going back thousands of years and in every part of the continent women were the basket makers.

Baskets
Everywhere

Not only in the Northeast where Yawata lived but in every part of the country, women made baskets. It was a craft dating back thousands of years to ancient times, when women tried to ease their household work. They became inventive, and made practical products out of the raw materials they found in nature.

They pulled together tall grasses and twigs and interlaced them. To carry babies, they wove material into backpacks and cradles. To transport water, they made water buckets. To prepare and serve food, they made cooking vessels, containers, and dishes. And just as women were able to find edible berries, roots, and nuts, so were they adept at gathering grasses, plant stems, leaves, or whatever was handy, for the weaving process.

Everywhere women found material for basketry. No region escaped their searching eyes, whether they lived in mountain cliffs, canyon valleys, or on fertile plains; whether they were nomads wandering from place to

21

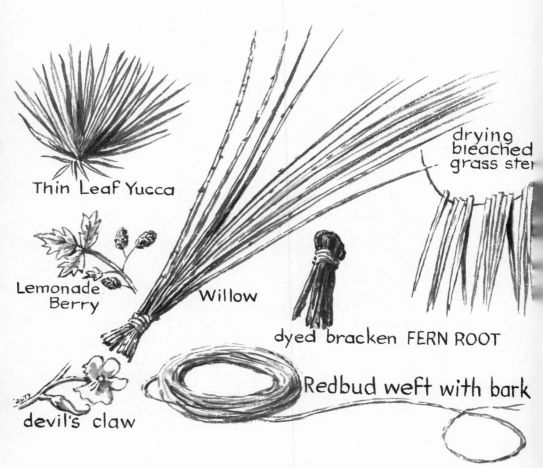

Thin Leaf Yucca

Lemonade Berry

Willow

drying bleached grass ste[r]

dyed bracken FERN ROOT

devil's claw

Redbud weft with bark

BASKET WEAVING MATERIALS

place or were settled near lakes and rivers. Even the desert yielded its scrubby plants, the prickly pear and mesquite.

Women learned from experience the best season to collect material. They gathered what they needed and bundled it to be worked on when they had time. They also devised processes for transforming tough fibers into flexible strands. It was hard, tedious work, but they persevered.

Their strong hands were their best tools, but women also used their teeth to crack away the woody coverings over inner fibers. Or they softened tough twigs by steaming or soaking them in hot water. Some women buried twigs in damp earth for several days to make them pliant. The most common tools were stone or bone knives and awls. They used knives to cut and shape grasses and twigs. The awl, a pointed instrument, was used in the weaving process to punch holes for the interlacing of different strands of material.

For many women it was not enough to turn out only functional objects. They created beautiful baskets, ones in which they expressed their feelings and thoughts. In doing so, basketry was both a practical craft and an artistic expression. They devised many ways to do this by varying both structure and design.

Women wove designs into baskets with different widths and textured fibers. Or they made dyes from plants, tree bark, and berries, and interwove red, blue, yellow, or black strands. They created geometric patterns or deftly wove images of birds, flowers, and animals. Some ornamented baskets with dyed quills, feathers, leather fringe, or shell beads.

No school taught these skills. Nor were techniques and patterns written up in books or pinned on walls.

23

The skill, springing from necessity, was stowed in the collective memories of the people and taught by mothers to daughters over thousands of years.

The craft was not studied only by a few but learned by women generally and practiced communally. It was a household industry. Wherever women gathered together they would pick up their basket work, indoors in rain or snow, outdoors in the sun; while they watched children, talked to friends, or cooked over the fire. It was part of the day's work, for baskets were fragile, easily damaged, and had to be replaced.

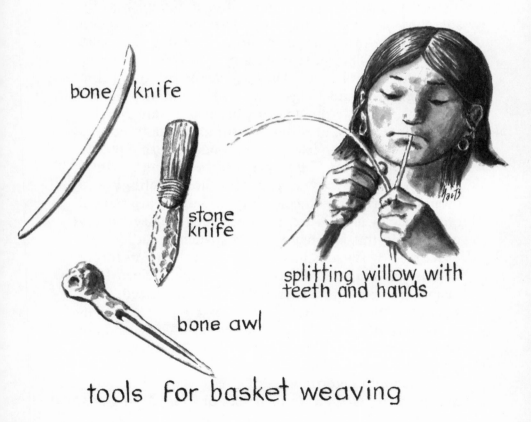

bone knife

stone knife

bone awl

splitting willow with teeth and hands

tools for basket weaving

PIMA BASKET MAKERS

For the very gifted, basketry was a special art.
These women searched for rare materials and worked
out new techniques and patterns.

When working, most women sat on the ground with
feet tucked in underneath, the basket on their laps. A
few sat with feet stretched out in front. Others were
comfortable in a kneeling position. Some even sat with
their knees raised under their chins, their hands cir-
cling their knees, free to do basketry. That was the

preferred position of the Tlingit women of southern Alaska who were among the great basket makers. The Tlingit made baskets out of spruce roots. Their Aleut neighbors used shredded grasses.

BASKETS

Aleut

Tlingit

Pomo Feather

Other great basket makers lived in southern Arizona where the Pima created geometric patterns out of local plants like tisal willow, squaw weed, and devil's claw. In northern Arizona, the Hopi made colorful designs out of sumac twigs, yucca, and willow. The Pomo along the Pacific coast made extraordinary baskets decorated with feathers. And even in the barren lands of Death Valley, women found material to create finely woven products, while the bold and adventurous Apache used basketry to express their dynamic spirit.

What started out as a simple method of webbing or interweaving a few twigs and grasses developed over thousands of years into sophisticated and varied skills. A popular basket technique was *coiling*, a continuous pattern in which leaves or splints were wound or coiled around other material which might be grass or wood rods. There was also *twining*, in which two or more horizontal elements were twisted around rigid vertical material. Basic techniques had many variations that gave novelty to the finished products.

By using the specific materials at hand, the people of each region of the country became known for their unique style of basketry.

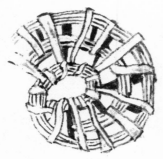

COILING

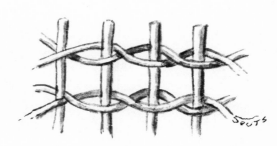

TWINING

"The
White Man's Ship"

Special to the Northeast and to the New England region where Yawata lived was the use of tree bark to make practical articles. These items were often put together quickly for immediate use and then discarded. They came in handy at sugaring time when families needed containers to collect sap.

"Barking" was done in the spring when villagers camped out to tap the maple trees. The preferred tree was white birch, though usable bark also came from the elm, chestnut, oak, fir, and cedar.

In a traditional technique, a standing tree was encircled with two cuts ranging in width from a few inches to three or four feet. A third cut ran up the tree trunk to connect the other two. Sometimes a tall tree was cut down. Then using strong sticks or chisel-shaped tools, men and women pried the bark from the tree trunk. To make the heavy outer bark more pliable, it was beaten with a woodheaded hammer called a maul. Other bark was softened by soaking in hot water. Out of now pliant bark, Yawata and other women made not only

TREE BARKING

buckets for maple syrup but also cradles, utensils, cups, and even pots that could be hung over steaming stones and used for cooking.

The bark was folded over into a required object and stitched together with split spruce or cedar roots, though the hemp plant provided the strongest thread. Women twisted hemp fibers on their bare thighs to make them thin and strong.

Early European explorers and traders, who had been making incursions into the region for many years, commented on the variety of woven and bark articles they found. The English missionary Daniel Gookin wrote (years later) about his surprise at finding baskets made of "maise husks, others of a kind of silk grass, others of a kind of wild hemp, and some of bark of trees. Many of these are very neat . . . with the portraitures of birds, beasts, fishes, and flowers upon them in color."

To ornament her baskets and bark objects, Yawata used berries for dyes. She also made other colors from minerals in the soil. Graphite gave her the color black; ocher produced red and yellow.

Yellow! Yawata looked again at the sunflowers. She had to gather the yellow sun petals for a dye. She would also use the sunflower stems in basketry even though the fibers were so fine that they did not show. But like corn husks, they were soft and provided a natural color. She looked at the rushes she had gathered in August and at the sweet grasses drying.

The sunflowers alone would keep her busy all fall. The disk of seeds, or achenes, would soon be ripe for picking. They were tightly packed against each other as if placed there by hand. She served the seeds as they were, to be cracked open and eaten; or she stored

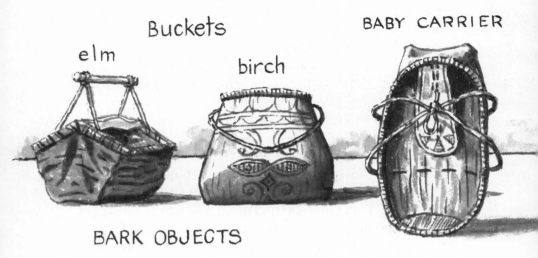

elm

Buckets

birch

BABY CARRIER

BARK OBJECTS

them. Often she beat them into a flour and paste for break and cakes.

Yawata had planted sunflowers not only because they were bright against the northern woods, but because every part of the plant was valuable. In themselves, the seeds were a food; the petals made a yellow dye; stalks were used in basketry. But above all, sunflower seeds made a precious oil when they were pounded into a mass and thrown into boiling water. At the point when oil floated on top of the kettle in large quantities, the water was cooled and the oil skimmed off. It was used as a food seasoning, a hair tonic, or as a base for the pigments that people painted on their faces for religious dances.

All around Yawata that autumn were familiar sights and sounds. Late corn was spread out in the sun to dry. Small animals were running through the ground

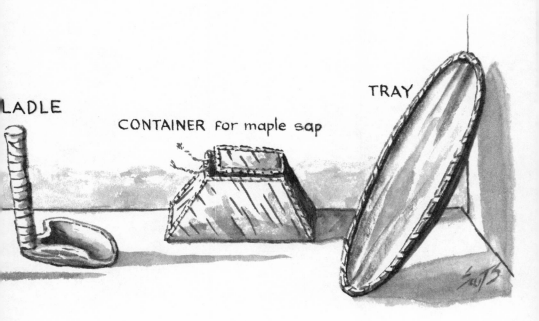

LADLE

CONTAINER for maple sap

TRAY

grass and up the trees, children scampering after them. But Yawata was uneasy as she thought about dismantling her summer home. And she knew why.

Kitonuck—"the white man's ship"—lay at anchor off the coast. It was another of many large wooden vessels with heavy canvas sails that had landed in recent months. On these boats came a strange people wearing strange clothes, speaking an unfamiliar language.

Yawata, like all the village people for miles around, knew about these strangers. She had seen them and also had heard about the explorers, traders, and sailors who had visited the villages. As a result of their visits, terrible things had happened. There had been violent skirmishes along the coast in which Indians had been kidnapped and a few sold into slavery. Worst of all was the spread of diseases common in Europe but

33

to which the native people had developed no immunity. Diseases such as smallpox, plague, and measles swept through the villages. In 1616 and 1617 a terrible epidemic ran rampant along the coast, devastating whole villages of people including the Wampanoag. It may have been the plague or typhoid, but the native population had no experience with such pestilence and were unable to treat it. Among the thousands who died were hunters and warriors, leaving the villagers unprotected. And now some of these same strange people who had caused so much havoc had arrived and settled on the land nearby. Who were they? Who were these families of men, women, and children so like her own family and yet so different?

Yawata had not paid much attention to the stories that had circulated through the villages for the past few years. Her people had taught the newcomers how to live in the woodlands and how to plant corn. They taught them how to fish, how to build homes, and how to keep warm over the cold winter. A white child, lost in the wilderness, had been found by Yawata's people and returned to the parents. Yawata herself had used a metal pot that the village women had gotten in exchange for baskets. It was strong and did not break.

According to Yawata's way of thinking, there was room for everyone to share the land in common, to use its plants and fruits. But events were not developing that way, in the way of her people. She was worried. Though everything still looked the same, there was a

sense of foreboding, of great changes taking place. She feared the unknown, a people whose spirit was so different from hers.

Sometimes Yawata had a nightmare thought that she would not be able to return to her village in the spring, to her vegetable garden and the sunflowers. The earth she stood on was vital to her, it connected her to the world and was the foundation of her life. If ever she was separated from it, she would be desolate.

The Spinner

Mary Allen was just plain Mary to her friends. She was a slim, dark-haired woman whose sleep was still disturbed by dreams of her village back in England. It was only a few years ago that she, her husband, and four children had joined hundreds of others on an old sailing vessel that took them across the ocean to a new world.

During the day she was too busy to dream or to think back to her native land. Like the Indian woman, Yawata, her days were filled with responsibilities that kept her busy from morning to night.

In many ways Mary's life was easier than Yawata's. She did not move around seasonally but lived in one place. And Mary had the use of metal and iron utensils, pots, and pans that did not have to be constantly replaced. She had brought over from England bedding, small pieces of furniture, farm implements, and tools. Despite advantages, Mary's workday never ended. She raised the children, prepared and served food. She hauled wood and water from outdoors, churned butter, dipped candles, made soap, and planted a vegetable garden. She helped her husband on the farm during harvest and put up vegetables and meat for the winter. And all year round, in every spare moment, she was busy at the spinning wheel or the loom.

On Sundays, Mary and her family filed down the path to the village church to worship a single God in the ways of their religion.

Unlike Yawata who worked in a group of women, Mary worked alone in her home. Only on Sundays at church, or at village socials, did she get to sit and talk with friends. But Mary had a different set of values than Yawata and the Indian people. Though she worked hard for many reasons, it was especially important to make a success of the farm and fields. They were private property belonging to Mary and her hus-

band. All the newcomers felt the way Mary Allen did. They had a sense of individualism—of private ownership and private possessions. They traveled across the ocean so that they could own and farm land. Many had the use of domesticated animals. The horse pulled the plow; the cows, chickens, and hogs provided food. The sheep were shorn for wool. And to keep their animals from wandering onto other people's private land, fences appeared on the woodland landscape.

Newcomers changed the land in other ways too. The sounds they brought with them ruptured woodland silence, a silence that had long ago absorbed the beat of drums. Now roaring through the forests were musket shot fired by militia out on daily practice. There was the crash of iron axes felling trees, the clatter of a scythe hitting rock. On Sundays church bells rang out.

Mary and her family were soon joined by hundreds

of others. They all wanted land and so took over the
fields that once belonged to Yawata and her people.
From the thatched-roof log cabin that Mary had at first
lived in, she and the family moved into a large clap-
board house. She now had a huge downstairs room
that spanned the whole floor, and above was the
sleeping loft. The best part of the house was the vast
fireplace that became the center of the household.
Hanging from hooks or from a pole were pots and
pans. On the mantle stood candlesticks. The floor was
a clutter of short-legged pots and trivets for cooking
food over a bed of coals. Along the wall stood tubs for

salting meat and tubs for milk maturing into cheese. Near the hearth stood the spinning wheel. Though Mary had brought some clothes with her, they were patched and repatched. Cargo ships carrying clothing rarely arrived. Either they sank during stormy ocean crossings, or they were plundered by pirates.

At first Mary and other families had tried to wear the same soft leather clothes as the Indians, but they were accustomed to the feel of cloth. By the late 1630s most homes had spinning wheels.

Mary, like her mother and grandmother, was an expert at the wheel. She had grown up with it and at age

eight had taken her place in the family as a spinner. Now she was teaching the skill to her eight year old, Bridget. The more hands that worked the wheel, keeping it busy all day long, the more yarn for fabric for dresses, shirts, and linens.

But before Mary or Bridget could make yarn, there was the long tedious process of preparing flax or wool for the wheel. The process involved the whole family.

Mary had already selected a patch of ground for flax seed, and in early May, planting time, she scattered the seeds over the field so that they were close together.

Weeding started when the plants were three to four inches high. This turned out to be a delicate procedure because the plant stalks were fragile. To avoid crushing them, Mary and the children walked among the plants barefooted.

Plants were pulled up sometime at the end of June or early July when the lower portion of the stem had turned yellow. By then the plant had produced its delicate blue flower.

The purpose of the processing was to get at the fibers within the woody stem. The first step was to spread the plants out in the sun to dry for a day or two. Then came *rippling*. The flax stalks were drawn through an iron wire comb to break off the seeds. Like the Indians, they used every part of the plant. The seeds were either fed to cattle or turned into oil.

The next step was *retting* or rotting, a process of soaking plant fibers until they were fermented and could be separated. After the fibers were separated, they were again cleaned and spread out in the sun to dry.

Then came the *flax-breaker* with its long bars and beater to break the fibers down further. To separate the rough and short fibers from the long ones, they were *hackled* or put through a block of metal teeth. They were continously cleaned, separated, soaked, and combed. At last they were as thin as hairs and ready for the spinning wheel.

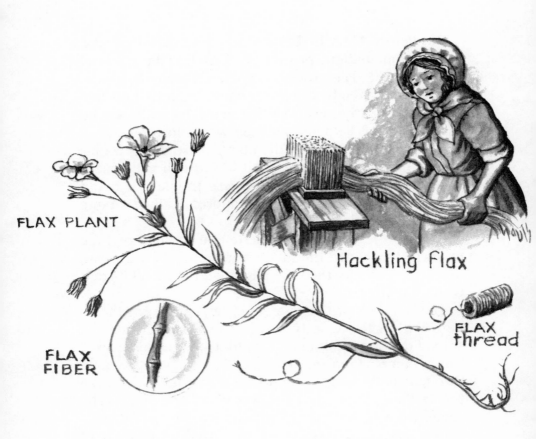

FLAX PLANT

Hackling Flax

FLAX FIBER

FLAX thread

Processing wool was much easier. Once a year, Mary watched her husband cut the rough curly wool from the sheep. Like flax, the wool was put through a process of cleaning, sorting, and combing or carding. Carding the wool by brushing it with combs that have strong metal teeth was easy but tiresome.

There was not time enough in the day or week for all the chores. At an early age, children did their share in the home and fields. At six years of age, they could be found bent over tables carding wool. In the average colonial family children did not have much time to play, and they were not educated at schools in reading and writing. Instead, they were educated at home in the practical matters of working on a farm, feeding cattle, and repairing tools.

Though Mary grabbed odd moments during the day to sit at the wheel, she really concentrated on spinning in the winter, from the month before Christmas until the spring planting season. From dawn to dusk the whir of the spinning wheel filled the home.

CARDING WOOL

The Distaff
and the Spindle

The purpose of spinning was to draw out, twist, and wind a mass of fibers into one continuous strand of yarn. Whether it was flax or wool, it was piled or wrapped onto the distaff of the spinning wheel. This was the stick or staff set into the table of the wheel. By turning the wheel, by hand or foot treadle, the fibers were drawn out of the mass and spun onto the spindle, a short tapering stick notched at one end.

Like basketry, the art of spinning goes back thousands of years. And like basketry, spinning was women's work, practiced by queens in their palaces and by the poor in simple homes.

Spinning yarn and weaving cloth were so basic to the well-being of a country that the distaff became the honored symbol of women's work. Images of the distaff and the spindle adorn old parchment scrolls and sculptured stone dating back to ancient Egypt, Babylonia, and Greece. For thousands of years, women did their spinning by hand. They are portrayed holding the distaff in one hand and winding the thread onto the

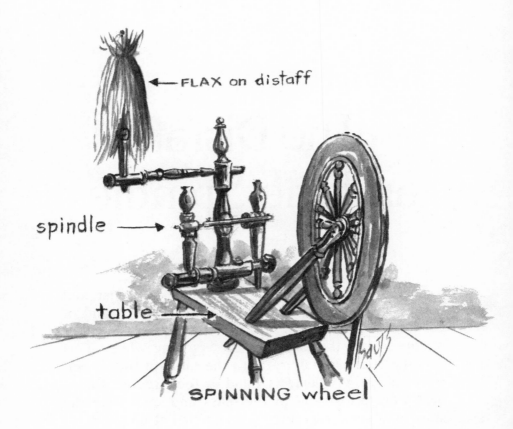

FLAX on distaff

spindle →

table →

SPINNING wheel

spindle held in the other hand. They did their spinning while occupied with other chores or while walking in the garden.

The Greek islands showed their respect for women's crafts by naming the great warrior goddess, Pallas Athene, the patron of spinning and weaving. Greek mythology also relates that the wondrous Helen of Troy was given a golden distaff. Poets were known to make gifts of ivory distaffs.

All over the great Eastern empires into the newly formed nation-states of Europe, women were the spinners. They made the cotton, flax, and woolen yarn that became the cloth for the dazzling costumes worn by kings and queens. Among ordinary people each family did its own spinning.

Only silk had a different producer. In Asia and Africa where the silkworm flourished, people learned to unwind the long delicate threads of silk that made up the cocoon.

Not until the fourteenth or fifteenth centuries did the nature of spinning change from a handcraft to a technological device. The spinning wheel put together the distaff and spindle into one mechanism. Though spinning at the wheel demanded as much time as hand spinning, women were able to produce more yarn.

In the cargo that came with colonial settlers, the Western world sent the spinning wheel over to the homeland of the Indian people. Mary Allen and others introduced the spinning wheel into the New England woodlands.

"Tomorrow Dances Behind the Sun..."

Yawata, the basket maker, and Mary Allen, the spinner, never met, though each knew about the other. In many ways it was a pity, for Yawata could have passed on to Mary valuable information about the riches and dangers of the woodlands. Mary could have given Yawata and her people the option of absorbing what they wanted from another way of life.

These two had so much in common. They were hardworking women, parents, and homemakers. Each was artistic and creative, the backbone of home and community.

But more drew them apart than pulled them together. They saw things differently. Their vision was formed by different experiences and needs.

Yawata felt she was part of the land she lived on with its abundant woods, flowers, and animals. The sky overhead and the brooks rippling through the woodlands were sources of joy. The very earth was vital to her life and her culture.

Mary, looking over the farmland, also loved it for its

abundant harvest, its flowers and trees. She loved the land not only for its beauty but because it belonged to her. It was hers. Her colonial neighbors enjoyed the same feeling of private ownership: the land and its fruits and berries were theirs. Fences marked off their fields from others.

Not only did Yawata and Mary have different ways of looking at things, but Mary arrived with the conviction that Europeans were superior to the native people, that she and Yawata were in no way equal. Such thinking made it easy for the colonists to push the native people around, to take over their land, and enforce European ideas by freely using their superior weapons, muskets, and rifles. The first years of trying to be friends gave way to violence.

Yawata and most of her people were wiped out. At first disease took its toll. Then came wars and murder. Yawata's descendants no longer made baskets in the same way.

Her people used cloth for clothing, metal pots for the household, blankets for warmth. Indian survivors of wars were often forced to become slaves. At one point colonial leaders put Indian women into a school to teach them spinning in order to relieve colonists of this tedious work.

Throughout the country so many Indians were killed that they were called the Vanishing Americans. But they did not vanish. Survivors held on to their long, arduous history and culture. They tenaciously regarded the earth as theirs. They struggled and demanded their rights. Today there are Indian scholars, writers, painters, and sculptors portraying their side of history, telling of their immense suffering.

There are also Indian women basket makers (joined

by a few Indian men) who work with their hands in the traditional way. Many are noted for the rare beauty of their work, and they can be found wherever Indians have settled, in the Northeast, the Northwest, or the Southwest.

Gracing the wide field of crafts are spinners. They enjoy the rhythm of the wheel and the feel of delicate yarn that will be made into rare pieces of cloth.

Today the basket maker and the spinner respect each other's craft and talent and each other's right to enjoy a different cultural heritage. They also recognize how much they have in common as women.

The Native American poet Peter Blue Cloud says it this way:

TOMORROW

We have wept the blood
of countless ages
as each of us raised high
the lance of hate. . . .
Now let us dry our tears
and learn the dance
and chant of the life cycle
tomorrow dances behind the sun
in sacred promise
of things to come for children
not yet born,
for ours is the potential of truly
lasting beauty
born of hope and shaped by deed.
Now let us lay the lance of hate
upon this soil.

Appendix

THE WAMPANOAG CALENDAR

The Months

(1) January, February

(2) February, March

(3) March, April

(4) Late April, Early May

(5) May, June

(6) June, July

The Moons

Squocheekeeswush, when the sun has the strength to thaw

Wapicummilcum, when ice in the river is gone

Namassack Keeswuch, the time of catching fish

Sequanankeeswush, when they set corn

Moonesquanimock, when the women weed corn

Towwakeeswosh, when they hill the corn

(7) July to late August	Matterllawawkeeswush, squash ripe, beans edible
(8) August, September	Neepunna Keeswosh, corn is edible; or Micheennee Keeswosh, everlasting flies
(9) September, October	Pohquitaqunk Keeswush, the "middle between" or Hawkswawney Taquontikeeswush, the harvest moon
(10) October, November	Pepewarr, white frost
(11) November, December	Quinne Keeswush, the long moon
(12) December, January	Papsaquoho, to about January 6; Lowatanassick, mid-winter; Paponakeeswush, winter month

Suggested Reading

Earle, A.M. *Child-Life in Colonial Days*. Darby, Pennsylvania: Arden Library, 1978.

Glubok, Shirley. *The Art of the Woodland Indians*. New York: Macmillan Publishing Co., Inc., 1976.

Handbook of the North American Indian, William C. Sturtevant, Gen. Ed. Vol. 15, Washington: Smithsonian Institution, 1978.

Lasky, Kathryn. *The Weaver's Gift*. New York: Frederick Warne, 1980.

Parker, Arthur C. *The Indian How Book*. New York: Dover, 1975.

Siegel, Beatrice. *A New Look at the Pilgrims, Why They Came to America*. New York: Walker and Co., 1977.

Warren, Ruth. *A Pictorial History of Women in America*. New York: Crown Publishers, Inc., 1975.

Welch, Martha McKeen. *Sunflower*. New York: Dodd Mead and Co., 1980.

Wilbur, C. Keith. *The New England Indians*. Connecticut: Globe Pequot Press, 1978.

NOTES

This book was written with the cooperation of many people but I would like to thank in particular Mary Davis, Librarian, the Museum of the American Indian Library in New York City, New York; and Ann McMullen, Curator, American Indian Archaeological Institute, Inc., in Washington, Connecticut.

The Wampanoag Indian Calendar is reprinted with the permission of Dr. Milton A. Travers, author of the book, *One of the Keys: The Wampanoag Indian Contribution 1676-1776-1976,* Dartmouth, Mass., 1975.

The poem, "Tomorrow", is reprinted with the permission of the author, Aroniawenrate/Peter Blue Cloud.

"Atisket atasket" is an old American nursery song that was titled *I Sent A Letter to My Love* when it appeared in 1879 in a book by A.H. Rosewig, *Nursery Songs and Games.*

58

Index

Hackling, 43, 44
Hammer. *See* maul
Hands, as weaving tool,
    23, 24
Helen of Troy, 48
Hemp, 31
Hoes, 15
Houses, 41–42
Hunters, 14, 18, 20, 34

Indians, 9, 10. *See also*
    Wampanoag
  Aleut, 26
  Apache, 27
  and basket making,
    10, 15, 21–27, 29,
    31, 51, 52, 54
  clothes of, 11–12, 41
  and corn, 18, 20
  headbands of, 11–14
  Hopi, 27
  lifestyle of, 14, 15–18,
    24
  mocussinass (mocca-
    sins), 14, 19
  Pima, 25, 27
  Pomo, 27
  Tlingit, 26
  tribes of Alaska, 26
  tribes of Arizona, 27
  tribes of Death Val-
    ley, 27

  tribes of New Eng-
    land, 10, 29, 49
  tribes of Pacific
    Coast, 27
  as "Vanishing Ameri-
    cans," 52
  women, 20, 37
Individualism, 39
Insects, 18

Kitonuck, 33
Knives,
  bone, 15, 23, 24
  stone, 15, 23, 24

Life styles, 14, 15, 18,
    29–32, 37, 38
Log cabins, 40
Loom, 38. *See also*
    spinning wheel

Maize. *See* corn
Manitou, 14
Mats, 19, 20
  cattail, 15
  and corn, 18, 20
  indoor, 15
Maul, 29
Measles, 34
Medicine Man. *See*
    Shaman
Mesquite, 23

61

Why Not Stay For Breakfast?

by

Penny Dann

First published in Great Britain 1986
by Elm Tree Books / Hamish Hamilton Ltd
27, Wrights Lane London W8 5TZ

Copyright © 1986 by Penny Dann

British Library Cataloguing in Publication Data

Dann, Penny
    Why not stay for breakfast?
    1. Breakfasts
    I. Title
    394.1'5   TX733

    ISBN   0-241-11926-X

Printed and bound in Spain by
Cayfosa Industria Gráfica, Barcelona.

Dedicated With
Love to
Jackie

Eating patterns evolve to fit around the working day, modern day breakfast, lunch and dinner together with elevenses, afternoon tea and supper are a fairly recent development, being characteristic of an industrial society.

The Saxon day was very different. They ate two meals, the first at around 9am. and the second in the afternoon. Their working day started and finished earlier since they depended on the hours of daylight.

'Breakfast' for them was likely to be cold pork, bread and ale. There was very little variety in the menu for the poor Saxons. Later, in Medieval times there may have been a pickled herring or two, beef, mutton or England's answer to Scots' porridge, frumenty, made from wheat.

What'll it be love

Menu

MONDAY - cold pork, ale, bread

TUESDAY - ale, bread, cold pork

WEDNESDAY - bread, cold pork, ale

THURSDAY - See Monday

FRIDAY - See Wednesday

SDAY - See

By Elizabeth I's reign they were tucking in to bread, cheese, bacon and beer. The Queen herself was known to like her beer.

Until the introduction of tea and coffee in the late 17th Century (and whilst they remained too expensive for most people) ales, wines and spirits were the usual accompaniment to breakfast. At Christ Church Hospital, London in 1704 the children drank beer in the mornings and in 1820 the Reverend Sydney Smith attended breakfast where the adults took tea, whilst the children drank wine! By the 1860's it was no longer the done thing to drink intoxicating liquor at such an early hour, except for the traditional tot at pre-hunt breakfasts. Victorian routine demanded that the family gather at 8am (woe betide any late-comer!) after an hour or so spent in letter-writing, music practise or exercise. The servants brought in the kedgeree, pheasant, eggs, mutton chops, sausages, muffins, toast, tea, coffee and chocolate.

"Mrs. Beeton's first book, appearing in 1861, acknowledges the existence of breakfast but does little more than suggest, in a few lines devoted to the subject, various ways of trapping the head of the family into consuming odd bits of meat disguised as rissoles."

Arnold Palmer - 'Movable Feasts' 1952

...finished! just in time for lunch my dear

In Britain the Industrial Revolution created a set working day for those in the mills, mines and factories. Breakfast became a necessity for as Palmer wrote, "the English stomach emits signs of distress after 4½ hours!"

Breakfasting on a grand scale continued amongst the wealthy who, during the early 19th Century maintained the two meal pattern of Medieval times.

Improvements in transport meant fresh foods from around the country and exotic new ones from abroad for those who could afford them.

Breakfast in a wealthy Edwardian household... Porridge and cream, coffee, China and Indian teas, eggs- poached and scrambled, bacon, ham, sausages, devilled kidneys, haddock, Kedgeree, A sideboard of cold meats... beef, partridge, pheasant, grouse, ptarmigan, galantine and tongue. Melons, peaches, nectarines, raspberries, scones, toast, honey, muffins and imported preserves. Phew!

During the Second World War tea, cornflakes, milk, butter, bacon, jam, sugar and eggs were all rationed, and just after the War bread was added to the list.

KIPPERS

Kippering is a method of curing that involves soaking the split and gutted fish in brine and smoking it over oak fires for several hours. Salmon were kippered as long ago as the 14th century, but it wasn't until the 19th century that a Northumbrian, John Woodger, perfected the process for herring.

In Britain, the main kippering areas are Seahouses on the N.E. coast, the Isle of Man, Great Yarmouth and the W. coast of Scotland around Loch Fyne.

Kippers can be grilled, poached, fried or jugged.

To Jug a Kipper: Put fish head down into a jug of boiling water and leave for 5-10 mins. Serve with butter, mustard and freshly ground black pepper.

"I don't know if you have ever noticed it, Jeeves, but a good, spirited kipper first thing in the morning seems to put heart into you"
P.G. Wodehouse - The Mating Season, 1949

Muffins made a regular appearance on Victorian and Edwardian breakfast tables. They were delivered each morning by the muffin man and kept warm by the fire.

Bone China muffin dish - early 20th cent.

In Britain today they are more likely to be eaten at tea-time but their popularity has declined. Arnold Palmer thought that the muffin may have become an extinct species! ...but "Prolonged and fruitless search in London and the Home Counties led me into down-

rightness; I should have known better. A muffin has recently been seen in Towcester, Northamptonshire. Fortunately, the Americans have taken them to their hearts, saving them from obscurity.

latest latest!

STOP PRESS MUFFIN SIGHTED

Breakfast in bed smacks of leisure and luxury........ In "The Young Visiters" of 1919, the author, nine year old Daisy Ashford, tells of her hero Mr. Salteena's excitement and delight at waking to find the footman bringing him a cup of tea and a biscuit....but he had to balance the tray on his "pointed knees".

He then dressed and went downstairs for his main breakfast of "steaming coffie" and "lovely kidnys".

In the 1920's the Countess of Suffolk breakfasted each morning on orange juice, Melba toast, black coffee and cigarettes, a "flimsy start to the day" commented Palmer.

Scotland

"The halesome parritch, chief o'Scotia's food" - Burns.

Oats have been grown for food since the Iron Age, and being a hardy cereal it fares well in Scotland's climate. The oats are dried, shelled and ground to produce the oatmeal used for porridge. The Scottish name for porridge is 'brochan', it is traditional to eat it (whilst standing up!) from a birchwood bowl, with a horn spoon, accompanied by porter - a type of beer, or skeachan - treacle ale. The Shetlanders have an oatmeal dish called "WIRTIGLUGS!"

Always stir your porridge clockwise!

esides porridge ... try
ring fried in a coating of
tmeal, warm milk dough baps
ith marmalade or
eather honey....

... A FINNAN HADDIE .... a haddock smoked over peat and moss fires in Findon, near Aberdeen. I am able to report that they are absolutely delicious since sampling one during breakfast at the Savoy...

Och ... I wish we had a fridge

or Dropscones, cooked on an iron griddle. This method of cooking developed from the hot stones used by the Gaels.

In the Scottish kitchen the oatmeal used to be packed into large wooden chests and the Mealy Pudding (a white sausage) was stored amongst it. This pudding is sliced and fried for breakfast.

Ireland

Ulster Fry (or 'Dead by 30')

fried, soda bread triangles (wheaten) (soft wholewheat bread)
treacle bread (wheaten with treacle)
potato bread (originally made to eke out the flour)
eggs, tomatoes, gammon,
black pudding, sausages,
bacon, and a big cup
of strong sweet
tea.

In Southern Ireland black pudding is known as DRISHEEN

Wales

Laverbread .... not bread at all but a Welsh breakfast dish made from seaweed. After hours of washing and boiling the seaweed is puréed, shaped, rolled in fine oatmeal and fried.

Perhaps the ultimate in English breakfasts is to be had at The Savoy, London. As breakfasters sit overlooking the Thames they are afforded the very best of attention.... tea or toast allowed to cool is immediately whisked away and replaced with fresh. It is an extremely difficult task choosing from the menu....

Fruit compôte?

A 3. or 4 minute egg?

Danish Pastries, Croissants or brioches?

apple, orange, tomato, grapefruit or prune juice? Tea, coffee, cocoa or chocolate?

crushed ice

Cereals and porridge with hot or cold milk or cream, brown or white sugar?

Omelette Nature?

Pancakes and maple syrup, kippers, finnan haddie, plaice, sausages, ham, steak, kidneys, liver, bacon, mushrooms or perhaps the cold buffet?

The Great British fry-up is often restricted to weekends and further still those unconcerned by calories and cholesterol! Still a little of what you fancy does you no harm, since a meal of cereal and milk, grilled bacon, fried egg and toast is quite well balanced nutritionally.

Transport cafés can provide breakfasts at most unbreakfast-like hours. At the Market Café in Brighton they serve their notorious "GUTBUSTER"... fried bread, eggs, mushrooms, chips, baked beans, sausage, burger, tomatoes, black pudding, steamed white bread and margarine, and tea from 11pm to 11am.

Bacon Butty

Crispy grilled bacon, tomato ketchup, two 'doorsteps' of bread... lightly toasted if desired.

Ssssh..... in England there are black pudding competitions! The exact recipes of the prize winning puds are a closely guarded secret, but the basic ingredients are pigs' blood, fat and spices.

BEST CELERY

TOP SECRET

Whereas coffee was said to induce chastity, another breakfast drink, chocolate, made from the cocoa bean enjoyed a reputation as a mild aphrodisiac. The cocoa bean was used by the Aztec Emperor Montezuma and his people to make a drink and as 'money'. The Spaniards discovered it on their conquests, and took the idea home. They tried to keep it a secret, but by 1700 chocolate houses had opened in France and London. New ways of processing the bean were developed, and powdered cocoa went on sale in America in 1827. Today, hot chocolate in Spain is sometimes flavoured with vanilla, as the Aztecs used to do. In Austria they add liqueurs and whipped cream.

Another breakfast aphrodisiac is marmalade. Well the Tudors thought so, especially, with their added ingredients, gold-leaf, powdered pearl, ginger and almonds, which they believed beneficial in such matters! Marmalade manufacturers today might still use ginger and almonds or perhaps add a liqueur.

Originally marmalade was made with quinces, the name comes from the Portuguese for quince - 'marmelo'. Orange marmalade was a 19th Century Scottish invention. Columbus brought oranges to Europe from the West Indies in 1493. Those now grown in the Seville area of Spain make very good marmalade.

Citrus fruits are now grown in many areas. In Australia and New Zealand where they enjoy a sweet marmalade the native crop includes citronelles, tangelos, mandarins and kumquats.

WITH ADDED GOLD-LEAF & POWDERED PEARL!

Ye Olde Tudor Marmalade

Warning

To The Consumer

The manufacturers accept no responsibility whatsoever for any incident that may occur after partaking of this preserve.

The meal immediately after the marriage ceremony is known as the 'Wedding Breakfast.'

A Victorian saying - "Never marry a man who does not eat a good breakfast. Perhaps it had something to do with the marmalade and hot chocolate, or that if he was eating he wasn't behind a newspaper, effectively halting any communication between husband and wife.

A.P. Herbert (1890 - 1971) wrote,

Give me a little ham and egg,
And let me be alone I beg,
Give me my tea, hot, sweet and weak,
Bring me 'The Times' and do not speak."

He also observed...
The critical period in matrimony is breakfast time"

Arnold Palmer suggests in "Moveable Feasts" that if a Victorian husband ate a hearty breakfast he could stay in the office for hours. Wives then had a lot of time to themselves. "The figures for divorce rose steeply" he wrote.

In 'Dombey & Son', Dickens describes a Christ-ening breakfast on a winter's day. All the dishes were cold and the champagne icy... Brrr!

"To open champagne at breakfast is premature, like uncovering the font at a wedding."

Pierce Synnott - 'A Wine and Food Bedside Book' 1972

Coffee

An Arabian goat-herd is said to have discovered coffee over 1,000 years ago. He noticed that a change came over his flock whenever they ate the berries... so he tried some!

In England coffee became the most popular alternative to alcohol. The first coffee tavern opened in Oxford in 1650, and they were soon all over London. At this time more coffee was drunk in England than in any other country.

During the Napoleonic Wars coffee was in short supply. Napoleon offered a prize for the best substitute. The winning suggestion used dried and roasted asparagus beans, ground and prepared in the usual way.

The taverns attracted the influential men of the day — Reynolds, Garrick, Johnson and Pepys gathered there. Since it cost only 1 or 2d to sit and discuss business, politics, the arts and philosophy amongst such men, the coffee-houses were nick-named the 'Penny Universities'.

Charles II became worried that these meetings were a threat to him and he tried to close the taverns down, but such was their popularity that he failed to do so.

Mind you, they were not that popular with the coffee drinkers' wives. In 1674 these 'coffee-widows' issued "The Humble Petition and Address of Several Thousands of Buxome Good-Women Languishing in Extremity of Want." In it they complained that their men-folk, once "the Ablest Performers in Christendom" had been ruined by coffee, and demanded heavy fines for male coffee drinkers under the age of sixty!

The men issued their own pamphlet, arguing that coffee was a positive boon to their sex-lives!

GOOD-WOMEN FIGHT THIS ENFEEBLING LIQUOR

Tea

Soon after their introduction both tea and coffee had their supporters and critics. In the 17th century tea was thought to be just the thing to induce a gentle vomit after over-indulgence! In 1797 a French visitor remarked "the tea is always excellent in England but nowhere do they drink worse coffee." William Cobbett (1762-1835) wrote an essay on "The Vice of Tea-Drinking". He also advised young men to "free themselves from the slavery of tea and coffee and other such slop-kettles" since they were time and money wasters.

In his tribute to Twining's Tea on the occasion of their 250th Anniversary, A.P. Herbert wrote

"Tea, (although employers think about it twice),
Is now a virtue rather than a vice."

The Virtues

Justice, Prudence, Temperance Fortitude & Tea

"Exhibit A m'lud"

Not only was tea-drinking frowned upon....

"Until the 19th century, no one ever thought of eating eggs and bacon for breakfast, and we now know that a large breakfast for an average man is a crime against his own body. Let us resist the blandishments of bacon, the charms (now noticeably faded) of the sausage. Devilled grouse wantonly superimposed on kedgeree, kidneys and bacon following the porridge in its facile descent, fish-cakes the size of billiard balls, above all the two or three slices of ham which so often rounded off the criminal proceedings."

(from The Times - 1950)

The not altogether serious "Anti-Teapot Society" was formed in 1864. They published a quarterly magazine, "The Anti-Teapot Review" (no.1 - May 1864) and met to discuss "Teapotism"... a hatred of teapots rather than tea. Members were also enlightened as to the leading features of the male and female teapot!

PLAYPOTS OF THE MONTH · May 1864

Dr. Samuel Johnson (1709 - 1784)

...was a well known tea fanatic. He once wrote...

"So hear it then my Rennie dear,
Nor hear it with a frown,
You cannot make the tea so fast
As I can gulp it down."

He frequently drank tea at Twining's, which was then a 'Coffee house' on the site of 216, The Strand, London. Twinings are still selling tea and coffee there today.

" It seems in some cases
kind nature hath planned,
That names with their callings agree,
For Twining the tea man that
lives in the Strand,
Would be 'Wining', deprived of his
T. "

Theodore Hook (1778 - 1841)

For breakfast Twining's recommend a "pungent malty assam" or a special breakfast blend, English, Irish, Ceylon, or Queen Mary.

In the 18th century there were no street numbers... Twining's shop was to be found at the sign of the Golden Lion.

coffee beans

TEA

Tea Drinker

Coffee Drinker

A 'typical' tea drinker is pictured as cheerful, middle-aged, nervous, fat, sociable, generous, old-fashioned.

Whereas a 'typical' coffee drinker would be intellectual, well-to-do, modern, middle-class, sophisticated. (Information taken from Coffee Council market research!)

The transatlantic cruise-liners had their heyday between the two World Wars. The breakfast menus on board these steam ships were vast. In 1935 the Cunard ship 'Lancastria' offered a choice of 13 fruits and compôtes, 12 cereals, 3 fish dishes, eggs and omelettes, 2 meat dishes with vegetables, hams, cutlets, kidneys and sausages from the grill, a cold buffet, 11 breads, muffins, griddle cakes, 6 jams, marmalade, honey, 5 teas, 2 types of coffee and various chocolate and malt drinks. Such a grand menu would have been on offer to the 1st class passengers, those travelling 3rd class on the 'Titanic' were given tripe and onions for breakfast.

From the late 17th Century stage coaching inns began to provide refreshments as well as accommodation. The coaches had very tight schedules though with only ten minutes allowed for breakfast. Imagine the indigestion suffered after rushing to consume pigeon pie, steak and kidneys!

19th Century rail travellers experienced similar problems. The trains had no refreshment facilites, so short stops were made at stations en route. However, by the time the passengers had been served they had to dash back to the train before it set off again. Things improved when the first restaurant car, providing lunches and dinners, was brought into service in 1879. A few years later breakfasts were served, even to third-class passengers.

Today breakfast is available on British Rail's Inter-City trains, orange juice, tea, coffee, cereals, porridge, mixed grill or fish, toast, croissants, bread rolls and a selection of marmalades.

One morning in February 1986 Her Majesty the Queen was traveling to London on board an Inte

ity train. Unfortunately her
British Rail breakfast failed to
appear for a whole hour....
The Royal passenger waited patient-
ly in one carriage, the Royal
repast was in another, the connect-
ing door was locked and no one
could find the key!

Eventually the train stopped
at a station and waiting com-
muters were surprised to see
extremely flustered stewards
dashing along the platform
bearing silver salvers of kippers,
eggs, bacon, toast, tea and coffee!

In t
half
20th Century tra
the height of sophisticat
exact! In April 1986 Conco
flight to New Zealand, and include
of Halley's Comet.. Breakfast was ser
ween London and Bahrain.... Champagne, fr
grilled tournedos steak, bacon and English st
sautéed mushrooms, tomatoes, asparagus spears :
wafer-thin pancakes with shrimp, scallop and scar
saffron flavoured cream sauce, buttered snow peas a
roll, butter and marmalade, cheeses and crackers, cof

France

"Few things bought with money are more delightful than a French breakfast"
N. P. Willis - "Pencillings by the Way" - 1835

Croque Monsieur.... dip two slices of bread into beaten egg. Sandwich a slice of ham and a slice of cheese between the bread and fry. *Croque Madame* is created by putting a fried egg on top.

The steaming bowls of café au lait and hot fresh croissants now so typically French have their origins in Eastern Europe...

the Turkish flag

The Turks attempted to invade Eastern Europe during the 17th century, inspired by this event, bakers in Budapest made crescent shaped rolls from bread dough with added milk and butter.

How to fold a croissant

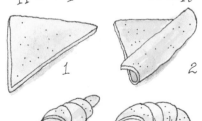

1

2

3

4

Austria

Vienna also came under Turkish siege for a time and, when the thwarted Turks retreated, they left behind the secret of good coffee. Today, 'Viennese blend' uses the Turkish idea of adding dried fig to the coffee.

The Viennese start work very early and take a light breakfast at about 6:30am, milchkafe, bread, marmalade, a boiled egg or a croissant (known as a kipferl). Later breakfasts are more substantial and include wurst of every kind.

A Greek breakfast... honeydew melon, creamy Greek yoghurt and a spiral of honey

With such a range of ethnic cultures you could eat your way around the world. However, in 'New-Yorkese'.... 'Eggs on a raft' sound far more exciting than eggs on toast.

Eggs 'over easy' or 'over light' means fried and turned, as opposed to 'sunny-side up'. 'English' muffins, bagels and cream cheese, semolina- served hot and runny or cold and set. Sweet things are very popular...

Coffee is consumed in vast quantities

DOUGHNUTS
- even doughnut holes!
- often flavoured, perhaps chocolate or blackcurrant

Danish pastries, stacks of pancakes, with maple syrup, cream and fruit. Strawberry and grape jellies are preferred to marmalade.

a 'dropped egg has been poached

Waffles...
In Medieval times waffles were reserved for special occasions such as grand banquets. The Pilgrim Fathers took the recipe with them to the New World where they are now far more popular than in Britain. They can be enjoyed with crushed fruit, maple syrup, or lemon juice and sugar, or as a savoury dish with eggs and bacon.

An L.A. Breakfast... herb tea, organically grown fresh fruit, dry wholewheat toast or a bran muffin with honey ....so healthy it makes you sick!

STAY COOL

China

Limber up with delicious paper-wrapped prawns if you're a bit out of practice with chopsticks.

Dim Sum is the collective name for the array of Chinese dishes eaten in the morning, although restaurants often serve it until late afternoon as it is so popular. I sampled my first Dim Sum at a restaurant in London's China Town.

It is served in little bowls and a tower of bamboo steamers with lots and lots of tea.

Dumplings..... prawn, pork, beef, meat (ominously vague) and shark's fin.

ther dishes include...
icken in steamed bread,
cy chicken and duck
et, Woo Kok - yam
quette, glutenous rice
apped in lotus leaves
d Lo Pak Ko - turnip
te! There are sweet dishes
if you can manage them...
haps sesame croquette, egg
t or Ma Lai Ko, described
ply as a "sweet pudding."

JAPAN

o fatty fry-ups for the Japanese,
IISOSHIRU a vegetable soup with
dried tunny fish, TSUKEMONO
- pickles, baked fish and rice.
ke the Welsh the Japanese eat
seaweed dish called NORI and
ey also love British marmalade!

RUSSIA

BLINIS - buckwheat and
wheatflour pancakes that would
no doubt fortify a Cossack eaten
with caviar - IKRA, and a glass or
two of vodka. The less warrior
like amongst us might enjoy
them for breakfast with sour
cream - SMETANA, and melted
butter, or bacon and a cup of
tea..... the Russians grow their
own tea in the State of Georgia.

Actually we'd rather like some toast

India

n the major Indian cities
s possible to find a familiar
itish breakfast' if you really
ant to. Far better though, to
ke advantage of all the
ative foods .... nan bread,
ce cakes, dahl, samosas and
ot chutney, oranges, papayas,
nikus, grapes, bananas or....

On Indian trains
breakfast is often
served on banana
leaves

KEDGEREE, that essential
part of the Victorian 'empire-
building' breakfast, was adapted
by British Colonials from the
Indian rice and pea dish –
KHITCHRI. The Anglicized version
uses rice and cooked fish
such as smoked haddock,
fried onion, turmeric, chopped
hard-boiled egg and perhaps
a little curry powder.

deep fried chillies!

In the book "Gulliver's Travels" Swift tells of
a war fought between those who broke their eggs at the
small end and those who cracked the big end. The
war raged for six and thirty moons and many
thousands lost their lives!

Take a saucepan and fill it with water, warm if possible so that it does not take quite so long to come to the boil as it would if it were cold. Now get an egg, preferably a fresh one and put it into the water, at the same time trying to avoid scalding your fingers. I forgot to say that the water must be boiling before you insert the egg.

One way I have found of putting in the egg withou burning my fingers and cracking the shell is to put it in with a spoon. Leave it in the boiling wate for a few minutes. You can never tell whether it's goir to be too soft or too hard That is one of the many mysteries of cooking. 99 by Sir John Betjeman. (1906 - 1984)

How to boil an egg

Devilled Eggs

...from the "Queen Cookery Book" - 1922
Place pieces of fried ham, dusted
with cayenne pepper into individual cocotte dishes.
Place poached eggs on top and
fill cases with 'devil' sauce.
SAUCE: 1-2 small onions chopped
and lightly fried, one pinch
cayenne, 1 teaspoon curry powder.
Fry the ingredients together for
a while, make some white sauce,
add to frying-pan with a little
Worcester sauce and heat through.

The writer also gives
Instructions for fried eggs...
When cooked they should be pl...
on a clean cloth
and carefully
trimmed'

A boiled
egg
'opener'!

FRAMED EGG

Use a pastry-cutter to cut a hole from the centre of a slice of bread. Fry the bread on one side, turn, break an egg into the hole and fry until both the egg and the bread are cooked.

Mirror Eggs

Butter a heat-proof dish, break an egg into it, and season. Cook in a hot oven for about 5 minutes.

I say, I say, I say, What did the Spanish farmer say to his hen?

OLÉ!

In our rush, many of us may go, as Sydney Smith put it in 1845 - "breakfastless"... but there's no excuse really; breakfast cereals can be prepared and eaten in no time. Cornflakes were invented during the late 19th Century by Dr. Kellogg of Battle Creek, Michigan U.S.A. There are so many brands of cereal on the market now, some more appetizing than others...

On Nevski Bridge a Russian stood, Chewing his beard for lack of food, Said he, "It's tough this stuff to eat, But a darn sight better than shredded wheat."

(Anon.)

A health conscious generation is now eating brown toast, low fat spread, natural yoghurt, fruit, bran and Dr. Bircher's invention Muesli

YOGHURT

MASS OBSERVATION (founded in 1937) aims
to make a record of every day life in Britain. They have
even investigated the modern breakfast, but don't worry....
you're not being watched! The information is gathered
from volunteers who write on a given subject 4 times a year.

The End

John Betjeman's 'Recipe for Boiling an Egg' reprinted by permission of Curtis Brown Ltd.
Copyright John Betjeman.
Extracts from "Movable Feasts" by Arnold Palmer, Oxford University Press 1952, by permission of Oxford University Press.

Books I found especially informative.....
"The Great British Breakfast." Ian Read and Maite Manjón, Michael Joseph, 1981.
"In Search of Food," D. and R. Mabey, MacDonald, 1978.

"The Piccolo Eating Book," Bronwen O'Connor, 1976.
"The Scots Kitchen," F. Marian McNeill, Blackie and Son Ltd. 1929.
"The Book of Marmalade," C. Anne Wilson, Constable, 1985.

Many thanks to all those who helped me in my research....
Bill Bingham, Anne and Lionel Barnard, Vic Amor, John Burr, Jackie Campbell, Jonathon Green, Tom Johnston, Mrs. Jones and Twinings, Mark Kaner, Sally Shread, Barbara Spitz, Graham Uden, Linda Whaley and Mr. Luigi Zambon.